MIDLOTHIAN

3 1614 0017 8049

P9-BZQ-861

I yam a donkey!

story, pictures,
and bad grammar
by CECE BELL

MIDLOTHIAN PUBLIC LIBRARY
147__ S. KENTON AVENUE
MIDLOTHIAN, IL 60445

CLARION BOOKS
Houghton Mifflin Harcourt
Boston New York

For Walter Robinson and Dennis Reaser—
you was both real good teachers

Clarion Books • 215 Park Avenue South • New York, New York 10003 • Copyright © 2015 by Cece Bell • All rights reserved. For information about permission to reproduce selections from this book, write to Permissions, Houghton Mifflin Harcourt Publishing Company, 215 Park Avenue South, New York, New York 10003. • Clarion Books is an imprint of Houghton Mifflin Harcourt Publishing Company. • www.hmhco.com • The illustrations in this book were done in china marker and acrylics on vellum. • The text was set in ITC American Typewriter Std Medium. • Library of Congress Cataloging-in-Publication Data • Bell, Cece, author, illustrator. • I yam a donkey / Cece Bell. • pages cm • Summary: Confusion abounds when a poorly spoken donkey says to a grammarian yam, "I Yam a Donkey!" • ISBN 978-0-544-08720-0 (hardcover) • [1. English language—Grammar—Fiction. 2. Donkeys—Fiction. 3. Yams—Fiction. 4. Humorous stories.] I. Title. • PZ7.B388915271am 2015 • [E]—dc23 • 2014021781
Manufactured in China • SCP 10 9 8 7 6 5 4 3 2 1 • 4500521229

So you **is** a donkey—you just said so! Let's hear your hee-haw, donkey!
No, no, no! **You** are a donkey. **I** am a yam.

You is a yam? I yam confused. Because I **know** I heard you say, "I yam a donkey."
Don't say "yam"! It's "**am**"! Am, am, **am!**

SNIFF!

You **sure** you is a donkey?
'Cause that's not like any hee-haw **I** ever heard!

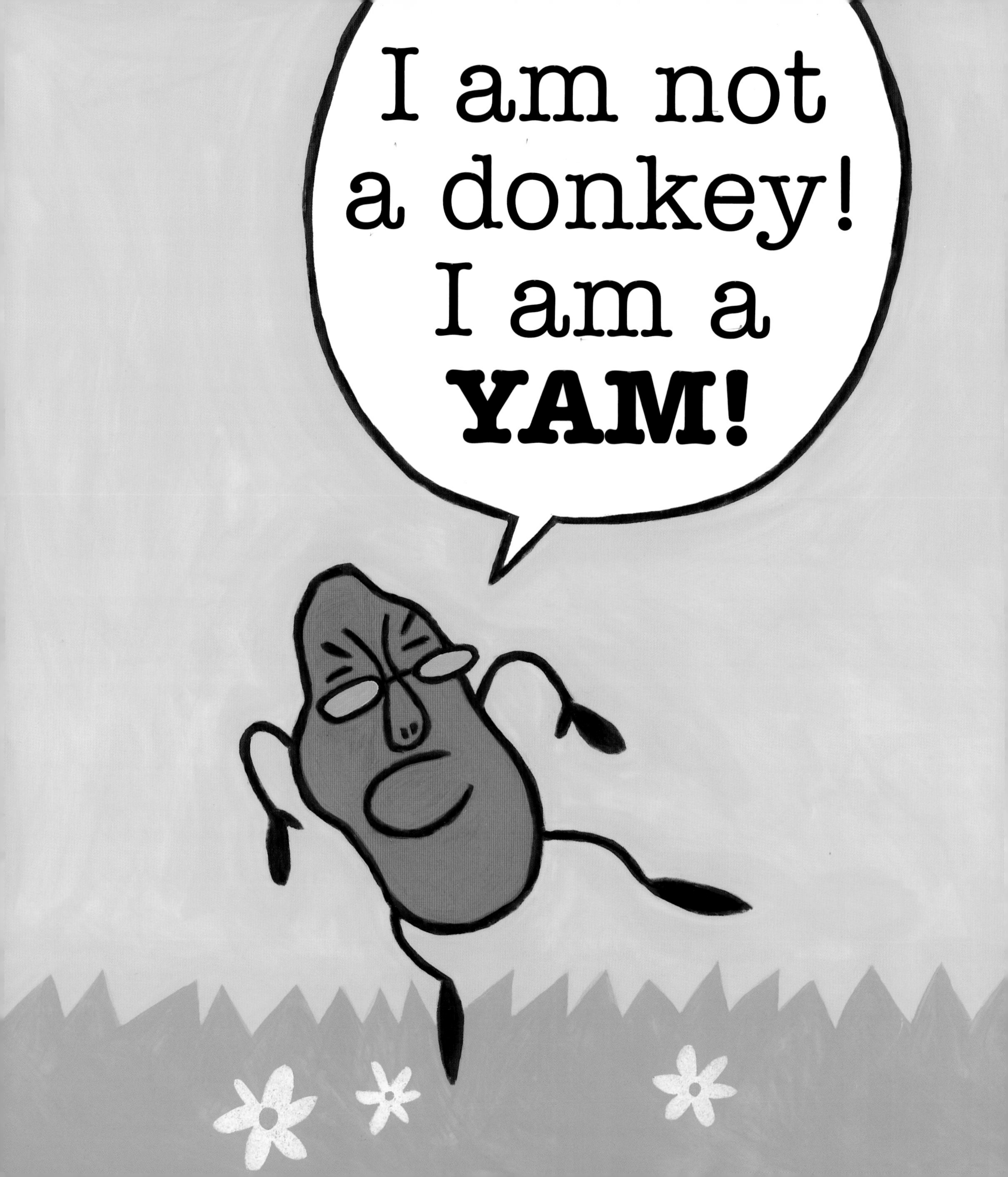
I am not a donkey! I am a **YAM!**

I yam confused.
First you say, "I yam a
donkey." Then you say,
"I yam a yam."
HEE-HAW! Yam-a-yam!
Yam-a-yam-a-ding-dong!
Whatever you is, you is
SILLY!

I have NEVER said "I yam" in my entire LIFE!
HEE-HAW! You just did! So what is you, then?

Oh, good grief. It's not "what is you"— it's "what **are** you." What are you, what are you, what **ARE** you!
Is **that** your hee-haw? You is the weirdest donkey!
What's going on?

Listen, donkey. I am a yam. It's not "I yam"—it's "I **am**." And you are a donkey. It's not "you is"—it's "you **are**."

HUH?

Looks like a big fight about grammar!

Is you trying to tell me that I yam not the only donkey here?
That you and all them other critters is donkeys, too? I need to get my eyes checked!

Oh, for Pete's sake! Look:
I **am** a yam. You **are** a donkey.
He **is** a carrot. She **is** a turnip.
They **are** green beans. Except
for you, we are not "critters."
We are **VEGETABLES!**

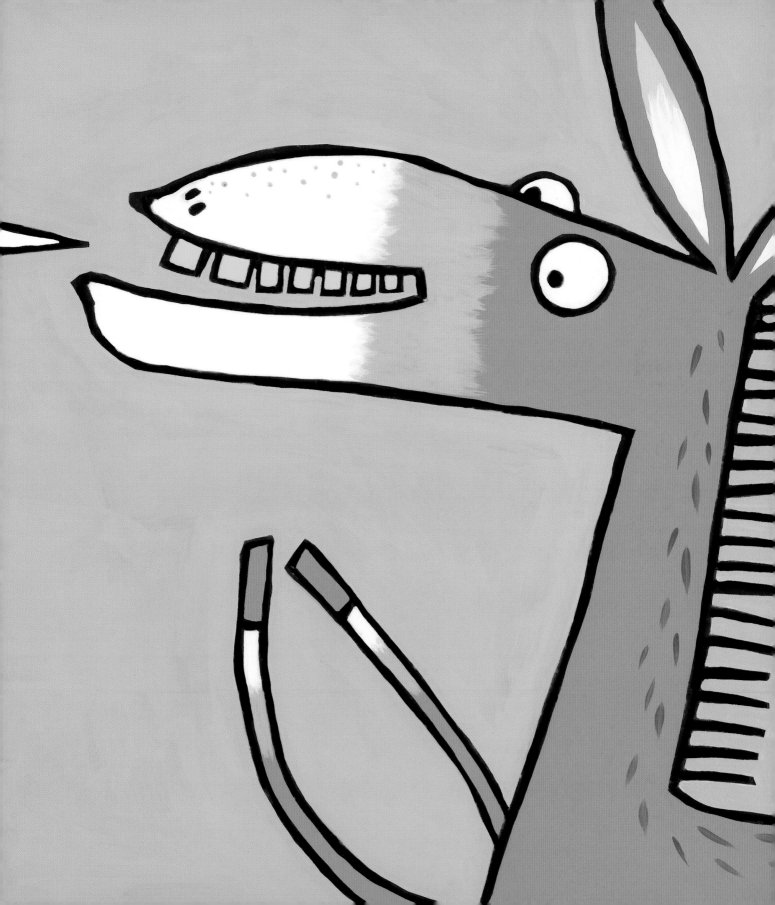